border to border · teen to teen · border to border · teen to teen · border to bor

KENYA

Teens in

by Rebecca Cantwell

Content Adviser: Angela N. Mwenda, M.Env.Sc.,
Lecturer, Christ the Teacher Institute for Education,
Tangaza College, Nairobi, Kenya

Reading Adviser: Peggy Ballard, Ph.D.,
College of Education,
Minnesota State University, Mankato

Compass Point Books ✦ Minneapolis, Minnesota

Compass Point Books
3109 West 50th Street, #115
Minneapolis, MN 55410

Editor: Julie Gassman
Designers: The Design Lab and Jaime Martens
Page Production: Bobbie Nuytten
Photo Researcher: The Design Lab
Cartographer: XNR Productions, Inc.
Library Consultant: Kathleen Baxter

Art Director: Jaime Martens
Creative Director: Keith Griffin
Editorial Director: Carol Jones
Managing Editor: Catherine Neitge

*The author sends special thanks to Barbara Muriungi, a Kenyan college student
living in the United States, for reading and commenting on the manuscript.*

Library of Congress Cataloging-in-Publication Data
Cantwell, Rebecca.
Teens in Kenya / by Rebecca Cantwell.
p. cm. — (Global connections)
Includes bibliographical references and index.
ISBN-13: 978-0-7565-2445-6 (library binding)
ISBN-10: 0-7565-2445-8 (library binding)
ISBN-13: 978-0-7565-3195-9 (paperback)
ISBN-10: 0-7565-3195-0 (paperback)

1. Teenagers—Kenya—Social conditions—Juvenile literature.
2. Teenagers—Kenya—Social life and customs—Juvenile literature.
3. Kenya—Social conditions—21st century—Juvenile literature.
4. Kenya—Social life and customs—21st century—Juvenile literature.
I. Title.
HQ799.K4C36 2007
305.235096762—dc22   2006027058

Visit Compass Point Books on the Internet at www.compasspointbooks.com
or e-mail your request to custserv@compasspointbooks.com.

Table of Contents

MOROCCO

Canary Islands

TUNISIA

ALGERIA

WESTERN SAHARA

MAURITANIA

MALI

NIGER

SENEGAL

GAMBIA

Niger

GUINEA BISSAU

GUINEA

BURKINA

BENIN

NIGERIA

SIERRA LEONE

IVORY COAST

TOGO

GHANA

LIBERIA

CAM

Amazon

EQUATORIAL GUINEA

SAO TOME & PRINCIPE

GA

ATLANTIC OCEAN

BRAZIL

Nairobi

Mediterranean Sea

CYPRUS
LEBANON
SYRIA
IRAQ
ISRAEL
JORDAN
KUWAIT
Euphrates
IRAN
AFGHANISTAN
PAKISTAN
Indus
NEPAL
BHUTAN
BANGLADESH
Ganges

EGYPT
Nile
Red Sea
SAUDI ARABIA
QATAR
U.A.E.
OMAN
Arabian Sea

CHAD
SUDAN
ERITREA
DJIBOUTI
YEMEN
SOMALIA
ETHIOPIA

CENTRAL AFRICAN REPUBLIC
UGANDA
KENYA
L. Victoria
TANZANIA
L. Malawi

ZAMBIA
Zambezi
MALAWI
MOZAMBIQUE

BOTSWANA
ZIMBABWE
Orange
SWAZILAND
LESOTHO
SOUTH AFRICA

LIFE FOR TEENS IN THE AFRICAN NATION OF KENYA VARIES DRAMATICALLY DEPENDING ON THEIR FAMILY SITUATION. A small minority live a comfortable life, attending well-maintained schools and enjoying access to computers, cell phones, and television. But the majority have a very different life. They live on the land in their traditional villages or in the sprawling slums of the major cities. In the countryside, students often walk miles to go to a school with dirt floors and only a few books. Millions of them have never seen a TV or a computer. In the slums, they may struggle to get enough food to eat and a comfortable place to sleep.

Kenya is a very young nation—43 percent of its population is 14 or under. This "cradle of humanity," as it is known, is also home to the remains of the most ancient of human ancestors. Kenya's teens are inheriting a country filled with promise and problems. The young people will decide what shape the future takes as the country moves forward in the 21st century.

The United Nations Children's Fund has supported schools in Kenya in a number of ways. It bought mosquito nets for the dorm rooms at Nagaa Girls Boarding School.

CHAPTER ONE

Hungry to Learn

A GROUP OF TEENAGE BOYS, each dressed in a white shirt and blue pants, pulls weeds in the garden plot outside their school. As the sun rises on another hot, dusty day, girls dressed in white blouses and navy skirts sweep their classroom's dirt floors.

The bell rings to signal the start of another school day. Students assemble for announcements; the raising of the black, red, and green striped national flag; the sing-ing of the national anthem; and a uniform check. Then they are off to class.

Kenyans have valued education since before the country won its indepen-dence from Britain in 1963. Under British rule, the native Kenyans were not allowed to go to British schools, so parents built their own. Since independence, the Kenyan government has promised to provide the first eight years of education free to all children.

Under British Rule

In about 1500, Europeans began arriving on the east African coast. By the 1800s, merchants, explorers, and missionaries were regular visitors. These European settlers began controlling life in parts of Africa. In 1886, Germany and Britain divided up the area, with Britain ruling what is now Kenya. The British took over large areas of the most fertile land. They forced Kenyans to work for them and, later, to fight with them in World Wars I and II.

Kenyans began expressing their unhappiness by the 1920s and formed organizations to protest British policies. Early in the movement, Jomo Kenyatta emerged as an important leader who tried to improve the lives of Kenyans. He and a group of his tribe, the Kikuyu, established a Kikuyu-language newspaper and independent schools for Kenyans.

A liberation group called the Mau Mau formed after World War II. The British responded by arresting thousands of African activists, including Kenyatta. Armed conflict between the Mau Mau and the British raged during the 1950s. A state of emergency was declared to place the country under military rule and suspend various civil rights. More than 13,000 Kenyans, mostly Kikuyu, were killed, while the Mau Mau killed about 100 British soldiers and residents.

The Kenyans wanted their freedom. They used the slogan "*Uhuru!*" which means "freedom" in Kiswahili, one of Kenya's national languages. Finally, as public opinion in Europe and the United States turned against colonialism, the British freed Kenyatta in 1961 and granted Kenya its independence in 1963.

Uhuru
(u-HOO-roo)

Following his release from prison, Jomo Kenyatta was greeted by supporters.

But when Kenya was a new country, the economy struggled. The government could not support public education, and parents had to pay high fees to cover the costs. It was 2003 before the promise of free education was honored by newly elected government officials.

When free education became a reality, the number of students in schools suddenly increased by 1.5 million. Students from families that couldn't afford the steep fees could finally realize their dream of going to school. But the sudden increase—especially in urban slum schools—posed major challenges. Many schools were already overcrowded and short of teachers and supplies. But teachers improvised, sometimes appointing a student leader to oversee the lessons of large groups. Books and even school supplies such as pencils were shared.

When free education became a reality, an 84-year-old grandfather started school to learn to read.

Teen Scenes

An eighth-grade girl finishes her chemistry experiment in the science laboratory. She walks across the manicured lawn to swim-team practice in the outdoor pool at her boarding school in a suburb of Mombasa, Kenya's second-biggest city. She meets with her friends, and they discuss plans to study together after supper. Next week she faces the three-day national exams that eighth graders are required to take. There's lots of last-minute studying to do. The young woman is already planning for her goal of getting accepted into one of Kenya's top universities.

Another teen, a boy, awakens to the sound of cattle in a nearby enclosure. He knows they are hungry and that it is time to take them to graze. He rises from his grass mat in his home in the *manyatta*, a traditional village of the Maasai people. To his people, the cattle are sacred. As a newly initiated *moran* (warrior), he spends his days guiding the herd from the thorn-tree corral to the rolling hills, making sure they are getting enough sweet grass to eat. While the cattle graze, the young man and his pals practice their spear-throwing skills.

In the city, a third adolescent wakes up to the stench of garbage in his tiny mud brick room and the rumbling and aching of his empty stomach. An orphan whose parents have both died of AIDS, he has no money for school expenses—or anything else. He lives in the sprawling slum of Kibera, near downtown Nairobi, where roughly 800,000 impoverished people live. Many of his pals have become "street boys," who spend their days begging. But this young man dreams of a better life and works hard assisting a shopkeeper who sells bread and milk from a small neighborhood shop.

These snapshots of what life might be like for three Kenyan teens illustrate how varied life is in the nation of about 35 million. Attending school is obviously not a given for teens in this country. For about 70 percent of Kenyan teens, formal education ends at age 12 or 13.

manyatta
(mun-YAHT-tah)

moran
(more-AN)

Ensheba Khareri, the head of a primary school, recalled the busy times following the abolition of school fees.

"With time, our shock gave way to optimism. We began to see ourselves as part of history in the making. We were giving children, many of them poor and marginalized, a priceless chance. They had a hunger to learn, you could see it in their eyes, and we were not about to let them down."

Today parents still help pay for school by purchasing uniforms and books. They also often pay registration and examination fees—an amount that can add up to 7,090 Kenyan shillings (U.S.$100) per year per child. This is a daunting expense for the majority of Kenyan families, which live on less than U.S.$1 a day.

About 1.7 million Kenyan children still do not go to school. In addition to the financial stresses families often face to pay for uniforms or exam fees, severe

Teacher strikes in Kenya are common, leaving the students to learn on their own.

15

A School Day

6 A.M. Wake up and wash.

6:30 A.M. Drink tea with milk and eat fried bread or toast for breakfast.

7 A.M. Walk to school, meet friends and visit, and help clean schoolroom and yard.

8 A.M. Line up for the bell. Uniforms are inspected and announcements made.

8:30–10:30 A.M. Class time: math, English, and Kiswahili.

10:30 A.M. Morning break: Play ball or swing with friends, and eat a snack of bread brought from home.

11 A.M. Class time: history and geography.

1 P.M. Lunchtime: School may provide cornmeal porridge and a vegetable stew, or students bring a similar lunch from home.

1:30 P.M. Afternoon class time: religious studies and arts and crafts.

3:10 P.M. Extra lessons: Computers, theater, sports, or clubs.

4 P.M. Teatime with a snack.

4:30 P.M. Walk home, wash uniform, and help clean house.

6 P.M. Complete homework.

7 P.M. Family dinnertime.

9 P.M. Bedtime.

drought in the mid-2000s increased the difficulty of keeping children in school. Some children were kept home to help their families search for water for the herds that represent a family's wealth. And some schools had a hard time supplying enough water for their students.

Because of the shortage of money for public schools, parents who can afford to do so often send their children to private or boarding schools that charge tuition. These are considered the best schools in the country.

International help is available for some of the public schools that are struggling. A variety of organizations are helping Kenya provide communities with funding to build new schools or purchase supplies. The United Nations Children's Fund (UNICEF) is one international group that supports education in Kenya.

The 8-4-4 System

Kenyans call their education system 8-4-4, meaning students go to eight years of primary school, followed by four years of high school and four years of college. At the end of the eighth year, students must pass a difficult national exam that includes tests in math, English, Kiswahili, science, religious education, and a combined test in geography, history, and civics. This exam determines who gets to go on to high school, so it is a major focus of the eighth-grade year.

Students must get a C to pass

and go on to a preparatory high school. Those who pass get the Kenya Certificate of Primary Education. The top students who score an A are qualified to attend one of the nation's best high schools, while provincial and district schools admit the B students. About half the students score below a C and go on to trade schools or start working.

Passing this exam is cause for great family celebration, and successful

Schools are commonly built with mud bricks.

students often receive a gift of money for the special achievement. However, even if they score well enough, some families need their teen students to start working. Only around 30 percent of Kenya's students attend school for four more years after age 12 or 13 to complete high school.

Fewer than half the girls finish primary school. If there are several children in a family, the boys usually get the first opportunity to continue their education. A mother in a downtown Nairobi market explained why she believes boys are a better choice for education: "A girl will not care for me. A boy is better than a girl."

Secondary Education

Kenyan teens who go to secondary schools attend what they call forms. In these grades, they study math, history, science, geography, and languages. In the upper forms, vocational subjects such as business and technical education are also included.

In rural areas with little money, the whole community gathers to create a *harambee* school. The term means "let's pull together" in Kiswahili and refers to a self-help movement that has been creating Kenyan schools since before

harambee
(hah-RAHM-bee)

independence. Villagers often make mud bricks to build a school building, and parents help build desks and raise money to buy books.

Kenya has seen a tremendous increase in secondary schools and enrollment since independence, largely because of the harambee school movement. In 1963 there were 151 secondary schools with about 30,000 students; now 620,000 students attend about 3,000 secondary schools.

Life at School & After

The school year runs from January until December and is divided into three terms of three months each, with a month off between the terms. Final exams are held the last two weeks of the school year. Primary school exams are mostly multiple-choice questions, with composition exams in literature courses. High school exams are a mix of essays and multiple-choice questions.

The school day generally lasts from 8 A.M. until 4 P.M. After-school activities for both boys and girls include football, called soccer in the United States. Students on a team might compete with other teams from their schools—dividing into green, red, blue, and yellow teams. The winning in-school team advances to compete against other schools. Other school sports include volleyball, track and field, tennis, hockey, basketball, and swimming. But Kenyan teens are encouraged to focus more on academics than sports.

Getting to School

One way for students to get to school in the cities of Kenya is on a *matatu*, a minibus. These privately owned shuttles usually carry 14 passengers. They used to be painted in bright colors with unique designs that often looked like urban graffiti. However, in recent years, they have become more standardized. Today they are likely to be white with a colored stripe of yellow, indicating their route.

matatu
(ma-TAT-oo)

Most matatus crisscross the cities on assigned routes, though some are more informal. A van owner may simply drive around, picking up and delivering passengers where they need to go. Sometimes they carry piles of cargo on their roofs as well. More than 25,000 matatus run on Kenya's roads and meet about 70 percent of the country's land transportation needs. Some matatus travel across the country, like a small bus service.

Matatus provide an inexpensive means of transportation.

19

In addition to sports, after-school activities include music clubs, in which teens audition to sing in the school choir. They perform songs ranging from Beatles tunes and popular U.S. musical numbers to traditional tribal songs. Still other students compete to make the debate club or poetry club, where they compete against other schools in academic contests.

Going to College

Another national exam determines who qualifies to go to one of the country's six public universities, and only about 2 percent of high school students qualify by earning the Kenya Certificate of Secondary Education. Students whose

In a unique school program in western Kenya, equal numbers of disabled and able-bodied students play football (soccer) together.

The University of Nairobi has more than 22,000 students, making it the largest university in Kenya.

families can afford it may attend a private university. Other students study a trade at a vocational school to train them for a career, or they start working.

Kenya's first university was the University of Nairobi, which opened in 1956, followed by Kenyatta University in 1972. Now there are six public and 13 private universities in the country, along with nearly 30 training colleges, an institute of special education, and three vocational schools. As with the other schools, public universities don't have enough space for everyone who qualifies to go, nor enough money for adequate computers or labs.

Even though going to school has its challenges, the education system in Kenya has succeeded in achieving a literacy rate of more than 85 percent, among the highest in Africa. As of 2003, it was estimated that 90.6 percent of males and 79.7 percent of females, ages 15 and older, could read and write.

21

In recent years, droughts throughout Kenya have made it difficult for herders to find water supplies for their animals.

2

Lives that Shape the Nation

AS IN MANY COUNTRIES AROUND THE WORLD, DAILY LIFE for teens in Kenya is closely tied to where the young people live and to their financial backgrounds. Teens from middle or higher economic classes are likely to devote their days to their education. They focus on their studies, and their daily labor is limited to washing their school uniform for the next day of classes and helping with simple chores, such as sweeping the house.

In contrast, rural teens are often expected to help with agricultural work. Inside the home, taking care of the basics of life can take up most of the day. Teen girls cook and help their mothers collect firewood and water, while young men watch over the animals and help their fathers in the fields.

Meeting Basic Needs

In rural areas, where about 70 percent of Kenyans still live, daily life revolves around collecting water and raising and preparing food. Running water isn't common, and teen girls or their mothers often have to carry drinking water in heavy pottery or plastic containers from a well, which may be about six miles (9.6 kilometers) away.

Other responsibilities of rural teenage girls include caring for younger children, the home, and the garden, as well as doing many of the agricultural chores. Instead of using a gas or electric stove, a traditional mother and her daughters usually cook over a wood fire and have to collect the wood to keep it burning. Just finding enough wood for the fire can take hours each day because, with rapidly increasing populations, many forested areas have been stripped of their wood. The phrase "a woman's work is never done" is used often in Kenya. From the time they wake

Younger children also help rural mothers and teen girls collect water.

Mud walls keep warm air in the home after temperatures cool at night.

until the time they go to sleep, women and teenage girls are busy.

Rural teenage boys in tribal groups such as the Maasai, Rendille, Samburu, and Turkana are likely to spend their days helping with the family herds of cattle, sheep, or camels. These tribes are nomadic or seminomadic and travel with their herds to areas where the grass is green or the watering holes are full.

Farmers, by contrast, spend their days working in the fields. They come home to houses that either are made of concrete blocks, with corrugated metal roofs, or are round huts of woven branches plastered in mud, with grass thatch roofs.

Heading for the City

As in other places around the world, young people in Kenya are increasingly heading for the city life. For women especially, opportunities there are greater. Urban women now represent one in three workers, one in three college students, and about half of the graduate students.

A Kenyan Hero

Kenyan women are inspired by Wangari Maathai, who started out planting trees and went on to become the first African woman to win the Nobel Peace Prize, in 2004. She is also the first to win the peace prize for championing an environmental cause.

Maathai is used to breaking barriers. In 1964, she became the first woman from east or central Africa to get a doctoral degree. She founded the Green Belt Movement in 1977. The organization grew into the biggest tree-planting movement in Africa. Maathai encouraged people to reclaim land that was becoming barren because trees were being cut down for development of farmland and homes. She taught women's groups to plant trees to conserve the environment and to improve their lives.

The Green Belt Movement grew into a campaign for education and jobs for women, and for other important issues. She opposed the dictatorial ways of the Moi government, which controlled Kenya from 1978 to 2002. Elected to Parliament in 2002, she later won a presidential appointment as assistant minister for the environment. Today she campaigns all over the world for environmental and social-justice causes.

Wangari Maathai accepted her Nobel Prize in Oslo, Norway.

Nairobi has a population of more than 2.1 million.

Teens from educated and wealthy Kenyan families in the city may live much like upper-class teens throughout the world, with big brick homes and expensive cars. Their parents may be doctors or lawyers or work for one of the Kenyan or international companies that have offices in Nairobi, the capital city. They are likely to attend boarding schools or private schools and are expected to take their studies very seriously. On the weekends, they may head to clubs with their friends, attend church-sponsored activities, or watch movies.

But for nearly 60 percent of the urban population, home is a slum, such as Kibera, near downtown Nairobi. Here 800,000 people live in shelters made from metal sheets, concrete, or wood and struggle to survive. Some of them work as cleaners or sweepers in businesses in Nairobi. Others collect cans and other metal to sell to recyclers. Still others run small roadside businesses. They buy food at a bigger market and sell it to their neighbors for slightly more money.

A Look at Language

Whether teens are from a farm family or urban dwellers, they are likely to speak Kiswahili, sometimes called Swahili. In addition to English, the language is spoken frequently in the cities.

A polluted stream flows through the Kibera slum in Nairobi.

The AIDS Crisis

In recent years, Kenya, like much of Africa, has suffered a major tragedy that has affected the lives of millions of people: the HIV/AIDS crisis. As of 2003, 1.2 million Kenyans were living with HIV/AIDS, and 150,000 died that year. About 900,000 children have been orphaned by AIDS.

This crisis has challenged Kenya in many ways. Grandparents, who traditionally would be looked after in their old age, are instead taking care of grandchildren whose parents have died of AIDS. The average life expectancy in Kenya has dropped from 57 years in 1990 to just under 49 in 2006 because of the epidemic.

A variety of programs, including education and counseling efforts, have been launched across Africa to try to slow the epidemic—and the infection rate appears to be slowing down. AIDS testing is a requirement now for admission to some universities and for positions in some corporations. Some universities and employers turn down those who test positive, but policies vary depending on the company. The scale of the disease's toll and its effects on the next generation will hinder Kenya for many years to come.

Life Expectancy in Kenya

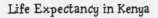

Life Expectancy at Birth (in years)		
57.7		
53.3		
50.7		
48.9		
48.3		
43.4		
40.9		

Year: 1955 1960 1970 1980 1990 2000 2006

Source: U.N. Common Database.

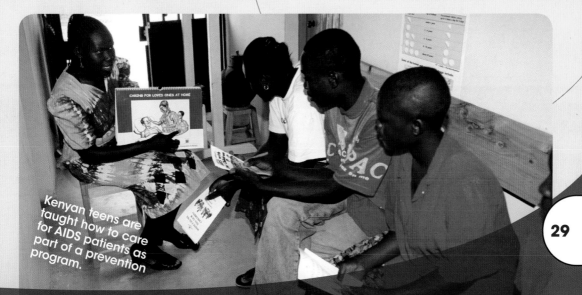

Kenyan teens are taught how to care for AIDS patients as part of a prevention program.

And though rural ethnic groups are more likely to use their own languages on a day-to-day basis, they often use Kiswahili to speak with members of other tribes. The majority of Kenya's teenagers speak three languages: their native tongue, English, and Kiswahili.

In a sign of the times, young Kenyans are creating their own language called Sheng. A street slang, it uses the grammar and sentence structure of Kiswahili but mixes in English words and sometimes words from Kenyan tribal languages as well. It has become popular among middle-class Kenyan teens, and it changes depending on who is doing the talking. Teens who like to talk in Sheng call someone who doesn't speak the slang a "Barbie," meaning a "softie."

The evolution of Sheng is partly a backlash against Kiswahili, one of the first African languages to be written down. Some Africans resent the language because rules for grammar and spelling were developed by white missionaries based on English rules. Kiswahili is known as a difficult language to speak properly, and relatively few books are written in the language. So speaking English—or mixing the two together to create Sheng—seems like a better idea to most young people.

The Foods of Kenya
Located on the equator, Kenya has a long growing season and fertile lands in the interior highlands. The country grows many kinds of fruits and vegetables, including such tropical fruits as pineapples, mangoes, papayas, and bananas. Many of the fruits and vegetables—along with fresh flowers—are important cash crops grown for export to Europe.

The main staple food in Kenya, as in many parts of Africa, is a type of stiff porridge that Kenyans call *ugali*.

ugali
(oo-GAH-lee)

Maize for ugali is ground with a large mortar and pestle.

A variety of vegetables are available at rural markets.

Women grind up maize, or corn, into fine meal or flour that is then cooked with water. The thick porridge is rolled into a ball and used as a spoon to pick up other parts of the meal, or it is simply eaten with the hands.

Sukuma wiki (collard greens) is grown in most Kenyan home gardens and is eaten with ugali. Depending on what's available, the ugali is also dipped in gravy or eaten with other cooked vegetables or, on special occasions, a piece of meat.

Other grains, including millet, cassava, and sorghum, are cooked into a hot cereal or porridge that is sometimes eaten instead of ugali. Rice is another common Kenyan dish.

sukuma wiki
(soo KOO-ma-WEE-kee)

Other popular dishes include *irio*, (a mixture of potatoes, corn, and peas), *githeri*, (maize and beans, perhaps mixed with meat and cabbage), and an Indian-style flat bread called *chapati*.

Kenyans eat goat, beef, lamb, chicken, and fish, but usually reserve meats for special occasions. Favorite meat dishes include samosas (fried triangle pastries stuffed with meat) and *nyama choma* (beef roasted over a fire or stewed.)

Some Kenyan tribes, especially the nomadic cattle herders, have a different diet. The Maasai, Rendille, Senguju, and Samburu eat a milk-and-cattle-blood mixture for most of their nourishment.

irio
(ee-ree-YO)

githeri
(gee-THERE-ee)

chapati
(chah-PAT-ee)

nyama choma
(NYA-ma CHO-ma)

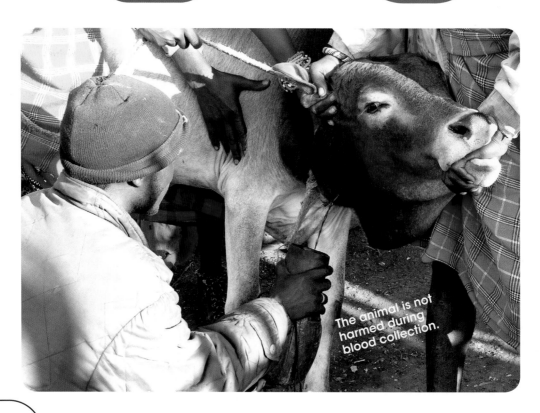

The animal is not harmed during blood collection.

They don't kill the cows, but puncture a vein and collect the blood in a gourd. The Turkana turn some of their herd's milk into ghee (a form of butter) and also make a cake out of milk, cattle blood, and berries. On the coastal areas and near lakes, Kenyans are likely to eat fish, including tilapia, made into a stew or cooked with coconut milk and rice.

Like teenagers everywhere, young Kenyans enjoy french fries, which they call "chips." Roasted corn on the cob, sold on the street, is another popular snack in the urban areas.

Corn on the cob is also sold at rural markets. It is roasted over small charcoal grills.

What's Cooking?

A typical daily menu for a middle-class Nairobi teen includes:

Breakfast
Chai—tea with milk
Chapati—fried bread or toast

Lunch
Ugali
Rice
Vegetables—such as stewed sukuma wiki

Dinner
Ugali
Cooked Cabbage

A Maasai woman greets her daughter, who has come from the city to attend a special tribal ceremony.

3

Parents & Peer Mates

SUNLIGHT STREAMS THROUGH THE DOOR of the mud hut as a rooster crows outside. The thick grass thatch roof gives off a sweet odor as the family stirs from their woven mattresses to begin a new day in their compound of small round houses.

Already the mother is heating water for chai, or tea, in the separate kitchen hut to start the day. The boys sleep in their own hut, while the girls sleep with their parents in the main house. For many Kenyans, family is at the heart of their culture.

Mothers at 15

A 2003 study reported that 25 percent of Kenyan girls ages 15 to 19 are either pregnant or are mothers. Though some experts feel this figure is inflated, teen pregnancy is a major problem in the country. Each year, an estimated 8,000 to 10,000 girls drop out of school because of pregnancy. The majority of teenage mothers are unemployed and have little knowledge of how to care for their babies.

One organization that is working to help teen mothers is the Teenage Mothers and Girls Association of Kenya (TEMAK) in the city of Kisumu. The TEMAK programs address the problems of HIV/AIDS-infected children, their parents, orphans, and the poor. Caroline, a teen mother of a baby girl, is one of the young women who found help at TEMAK.

"I joined TEMAK year 2005," she said. "Oh! What a wonderful place ... I am now back to school where TEMAK helps to meet my needs including paying my fees ... My dream is to be a lawyer."

Teen mothers also are at a high risk of contracting AIDS.

Focused on Extended Family

When Kenyan teens think of their family, they think of more than the immediate family unit of parents and children. The extended family—including aunts, uncles, grandparents, and cousins—is extremely important in Kenyan culture, and Kenyan teens often form close relationships with these more distant relatives. Kenyans in some ethnic groups call their mother's sister "younger mother" or "older mother," depending on the aunt's age. And they sometimes call their father's brother "younger father" or "older father."

In rural areas, households often include more than one generation. Grandparents might live in one home, while each son has a house nearby for his family. Because the average life expectancy at birth in Kenya is only 49, there are not many old people, and elders are treated with great respect for the wisdom they have gathered during a long life. Caring for aging parents is traditionally the job of the family's youngest adult son.

Kenyans come from nearly six dozen ethnic groups. Many of them still encourage large extended families to live next to one another on the family's traditional farm or grazing land. For example, several Kikuyu family groups may live together in one group of houses where everyone cooperates for the good of the group. Traditionally, several of these groups form another larger group called a *mbari*.

mbari
(em-BAHR-ee)

The Kikuyu people live in thatch roofed homes.

A Look at Ethnic Groups

Kenya's almost 35 million people belong to about 70 ethnic groups. Languages form the basis for most of the distinctions among the people. Social scientists use language groups to divide the Kenyans into three major groups: Bantu, Nilotic, and Cushitic.

Bantu speakers make up about 65 percent of Kenya's population and include the following tribes:

Kikuyu—_Among the first native Kenyans to encounter the white settlers in the 17th to 19th centuries, they soon adapted to Western ways. Most now dress in Western clothing. Independent Kenya's first leader, Jomo Kenyatta, was a Kikuyu, and many of the best government jobs went to Kikuyu people after Kenya won its freedom. This caused resentment among other ethnic groups. Today they make up 22 percent of Kenya's population._

Kamba—_These rural people were traditionally farmers and traders. Agriculture continues to be their primary work. The men often keep herds of cattle, sheep, or goats, while the women manage the home and care for the children. Today Kamba people make up 22 percent of the population._

Luhya—_About 18 subtribes in Kenya make up this group of agricultural people. In recent years significant numbers of Luhya have migrated to urban centers such as Nairobi, Kisumu, and Mombasa in search of work. They make up 14 percent of the total population._

Nilotic groups include:

Luo—_This ethnic group in Kenya makes up 12 percent of the population. During the years of British colonization, the Luo were forced to adopt Western dress and were taught English and European ways of life. In recent years, the AIDS crisis has struck the Luo people particularly hard._

Kalenjin—_This tribe, which makes up 10 percent of the population, traditionally farmed the highlands of the Great Rift Valley in western Kenya. About three-quarters of Kenya's famed long-distance runners are Kalenjin, as is the country's second president, Daniel arap Moi._

Maasai—_Though they make up just 1.5 percent of Kenyans, the Maasai are one of the most famous tribes. They are often portrayed as the face of Kenya for their distinctive clothing and elaborate beaded jewelry. Traditionally they worked as nomadic herders and hunters of lions. More Maasai are now settling on farms or in towns, or working in the tourist industry, teaching visitors about their culture._

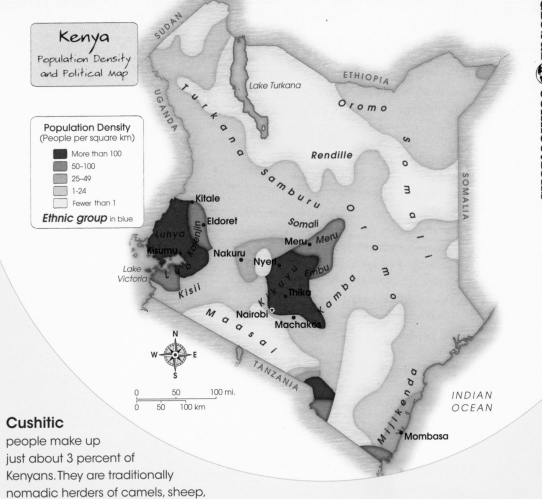

Kenya
Population Density and Political Map

Population Density
(People per square km)

- More than 100
- 50–100
- 25–49
- 1-24
- Fewer than 1

Ethnic group in blue

SUDAN

UGANDA

ETHIOPIA

Lake Turkana

Oromo

Turkana

Somali

Rendille

Samburu

Kitale

Eldoret

Somali

Luhya

Kalenjin

Meru • Meru

Kisumu

Nakuru

Nyeri

Kikuyu

Embu

Lake Victoria

Luo

Kisii

Thika

Kamba

Nairobi

Maasai

Machakos

SOMALIA

Oromo

N
W E
S

0   50   100 mi.
0   50   100 km

TANZANIA

Miji kenda

INDIAN OCEAN

Mombasa

Cushitic

people make up just about 3 percent of Kenyans. They are traditionally nomadic herders of camels, sheep, and cattle. They include descendants of people from Ethiopia called the Oromo and the descendants of people who came from Somalia.

Working Together

As in many other parts of Africa, divisions among ethnic groups have caused problems in Kenya. European colonialists drew the borders of many African nations without paying attention to who was already living there.

The first president after independence, the charismatic and revered leader Jomo Kenyatta, tried to stress the importance of everyone's thinking like Kenyans first, rather than like individual tribes, with his motto: "Harambee." While conflicts haven't been as bloody as in many other parts of Africa, Kenya has struggled with ethnic divisions. Nonetheless, Kenya has served an important role helping some of its neighbors, such as Somalia and Sudan, figure out how to bring peace to warring ethnic groups.

Peer Mates & Initiation

In addition to being part of a family, traditional Kenyan teens belong to an age set. The members of your age set, if you are a boy, are called peer mates, and include the other boys with whom you experience the initiation into adulthood. The puberty ceremony takes place between ages 12 and 15 and includes circumcision. In cities, doctors perform the operation. In villages and poor areas, an elder with traditional experience in the ceremony usually conducts the circumcision. The operation is not dangerous if done with proper hygiene.

In certain ethnic groups, boys go into seclusion before and after the operation. This symbolically shows that they have left their role as children and will return as young men. Special instructions from elders on how to take on the duties of men are included in the rituals of initiation for traditional groups.

Even urban Kenyan teen boys generally spend a month in seclusion from most of their family and friends after their circumcision, though they are sometimes with their peer mates. During this time, adults teach them about taking care of their elders, acting responsibly, and behaving properly. The end of the month of seclusion is marked with an elaborate family feast to signal that the boy has become a young man. The family might kill an animal and serve roasted meat, a rare treat.

In traditional Kenyan society, girls were also circumcised. That operation—much more severe than for boys—often caused physical and emotional trauma. Today the practice is known as genital mutilation.

As part of the circumcision ritual, boys sing about the bravery of those who show no emotions during the procedure.

The Battle Against FGM

Though the practice of female genital mutilation (FGM) in Kenya has significantly decreased in recent years, it is still performed in the majority of the country's 75 districts. However, the government continues to work with international groups, like UNICEF, to inform citizens about the risks of FGM.

Some of the most effective people to voice opposition to the practice are those who once performed the ceremony, normally well-respected older women in the community. They have spoken out against the practice even though it meant they would need to find new ways to support themselves.

Some of these women have begun organizing alternative rites of passage, which provide training to young women in their transition into adulthood. Others, like 80-year-old Isnino Shuria, have needed the support of their communities to help them find other means of earning income. Women in their communities have raised money so that these former practitioners can purchase livestock.

"There are about 25 of us [former FGM performers] now," said Shuria. "I [also] deliver babies and massage mothers who have problem pregnancies—it is much better. I have many well-wishers who help me and my family."

Girls at an alternative rite of passage learn about the risks of FGM.

41

In the 1990s, a worldwide campaign to end this practice helped persuade the government to pass laws saying girls cannot be circumcised under age 18.

The practice is still customary in some tribal groups but is increasingly opposed by women and the government. Traditional Kenyan girls are still initiated into a peer group and taught the duties of womanhood, and they move through stages of life with their initiation friends. In urban areas, female initiation is likely to be much less formal, with mothers sitting their daughters down to talk about the roles and responsibilities of women.

Dating & Marriage

In Kenya, it is far more likely for teen boys and girls to hang out together and attend church activities or school functions with groups of friends than to go out on one-on-one dates. Young men and women are more likely to be serious about dating after high school, either at a university or in the working world.

Young people today usually pick their marriage partners, but marriages are sometimes arranged by families, according to traditional custom. Once a man and a woman decide to marry, the negotiations begin for a dowry. The bride and groom—or their parents—each selects someone to act as a go-between. The go-between, often a favorite uncle, negotiates what the groom's family must pay for the bride through a dowry. The dowry is a way for the man's family to thank the woman's

A Friendly Nation

Kenyans are warm and friendly and like to ask about one another's family, sometimes greeting each other in ways that are distinct to certain age groups and situations. For example, Maasai children greet older people with a slight bow, and the adults respond by putting an open hand on the child's head.

Kenyans spend a lot of time visiting with friends and extended family, especially on Sunday, a popular day to drop in on friends. Afternoon tea is a popular time to visit, and hosts always give their guests a hot cup. Visitors usually bring a small gift in a woven bag—possibly tea leaves, sugar, cornmeal, or milk. The host is expected to give back the woven bag with a gift as well—perhaps bananas from the garden.

The traditional wedding attire of a Samburu bride

family and to compensate them for her loss, because after marriage, she joins his family.

Traditionally, the negotiated payment is in cattle or other livestock, although today cash or other goods have taken the place of animals in some places, especially in urban areas. Often the amount paid is top-secret—even some of the bride's family members may not know what is paid.

Kenyan men traditionally married more than one woman. The man would be expected to provide a different home for each wife and her children. But because of the expense and changing culture, multiple marriages are growing less common.

Traditional drummers perform as part of Nairobi's Jamhuri Day celebration.

4

Celebrating Kenyans & Country

AFTER DECADES OF COLONIAL RULE BY BRITAIN, it is no surprise that Kenyans enjoy spirited celebrations in honor of their independence. The country has three main political holidays. Madaraka Day, on June 1, celebrates the anniversary of self-government. Kenyatta Day is the anniversary of the first president's arrest by the British before independence was won. It is celebrated on October 20. And Jamhuri Day, also known as Uhuru Day, on December 12, celebrates the establishment of independence.

For Love of Country

Jamhuri Day brings a national celebration to Nyayo National Stadium in Nairobi. Teenagers from schools all over the city audition to participate in a special choir that sings for the event.

In addition to the choir, a line of young men march into the crowded stadium, pounding drums in unison. At the same time, lines of women wrapped in *kangas*—bold, colorful cloths— dance in behind them.

kangas
(kan-GUHS)

The performers join rows of military dignitaries onstage: navy officers in white, army officers in red, and air force officers in dark blue—all wearing gold medals on their chests. Politicians give speeches, urging Kenyans to work to build their country. And the crowd joins in singing patriotic songs.

After the ceremony, Kenyan families return home and the feasting begins, with roasted meats and fried breads highlighting the offerings at big barbecuelike neighborhood parties.

While assemblies, parades, dances, and feasts are common ways to celebrate the national holidays within the country, even far-flung Kenyans get into the partying. In 2004, Kenyans in the United Kingdom held their first Madaraka Day celebration.

National Holidays

January 1
New Year's Day

May 1
Labor Day honors the contributions of workers.

June 1
Madaraka Day celebrates the beginning of self-government in 1960, before full independence was granted.

October 20
Kenyatta Day marks the day that national independence leader Jomo Kenyatta was arrested by British colonial authorities.

December 12
Uhuru/Jamhuri Day marks the anniversary of Kenya's official independence from Britain in 1963.

Christian Holidays
Kenyans also celebrate a number of religious holidays.

On Madaraka Day, Kenyans attend public performances to celebrate their pride in being Kenyans.

Religion in Kenya

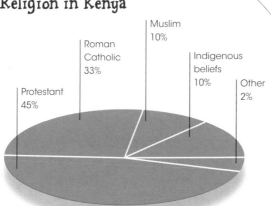

Protestant 45%

Roman Catholic 33%

Muslim 10%

Indigenous beliefs 10%

Other 2%

Source: United States Central Intelligence Agency.
The World Factbook—Kenya.

Kenya's constitution guarantees freedom of religion, and most Kenyans are respectful of other religions. The majority of Kenyans are Christians, with about 45 percent belonging to Protestant denominations and about 33 percent practicing Roman Catholicism.

For Kenyan Christians, Easter and Christmas are the biggest holidays, as for Christians around the world. At Christmas, Kenyan teens gather in churches with their families to hear sermons and sing hymns. The service is

On Palm Sunday, the week before Easter, residents in some communities walk through the streets holding palms.

followed by a family or village feast of fresh-roasted goat. Kenyans don't have a tradition of gift-giving on Christmas, but children and teens are likely to get a new set of clothes to wear for Christmas Day services. Poor people are served free Christmas meals by charities, and groups travel through neighborhoods singing carols and collecting money to give to their churches.

At Easter time, Good Friday and Easter Monday are public holidays, so the celebration and prayers last for four days. Many Kenyans take advantage of the four-day holiday to travel to their traditional village homes to visit and celebrate with extended family.

While the majority of Kenyans call themselves Christians, their independent African churches often allow them to combine Christian faith with parts of their older traditional beliefs.

Indigenous Beliefs

About 10 percent of Kenyans still follow traditional indigenous African beliefs. While their practices vary, they generally pray to one God, who is often accessed through the ancestors. Some Kenyans believe that God is most present in a particular place, such as Mount Kenya or Lake Victoria. Among those who still follow traditional religions are the Turkana, who call God Akug and believe he is responsible for bringing the rain. The Kikuyu call God Ngai, which means "divider of gifts among people." Maasai religious leaders called *laibons* are a combination of healers and priests. They are still consulted for their vast knowledge of the medicinal uses of plants and their ability to heal using these plants.

laibons
(lie-BOHNS)

A variety of ceremonies, such as animal sacrifice, are performed by followers of indigenous beliefs.

The sacrifice of a goat is one example. In many traditional African faiths, dead ancestors are honored by animal sacrifice. Some Kenyans believe the ancestors can provide help or advice from the other world, and the sacrifice—or, alternatively, offerings to charity—is a way to maintain contact with them.

Other major world religions, including Buddhism, Hinduism, and Islam, are also represented in Kenya. About 10 percent of the population practices Islam, which arrived on the coast of eastern Africa in the ninth century—about 1,000 years before Christianity appeared in Africa. Kenyan

Muslims recognize the two major Islamic holidays: Id al-Fitr, which celebrates the end of Ramadan, a month of fasting from daybreak to sunset for Muslims; and Id al-Adha, which marks the sacrificing of animals at the end of the pilgrimage to Mecca.

Another Kenyan Muslim celebration attracts people from far and wide. On the island of Lamu, the birthday of the prophet Muhammad is celebrated as Maulidi, with a week of ceremonies and feasting. The festivities include ritual sword fights along with lots of dancing. The special celebration was launched by an Arab scholar named

The stick dance is performed at a Maulidi celebration.

Death Customs

Death customs in Kenya vary. Many Kenyans are buried on their family's traditional land within two weeks of death. Often friends gather for a week to console the family, prepare food, and help raise money to transport the body to the traditional village where the burial site is located. Funeral feasts can be very elaborate, with a wide variety of food.

The funeral services vary depending on religious practices. Christian funerals involve services at a church and prayers at the burial site. Muslims wash and wrap the body in a white shroud and then take it to the mosque for prayers before burial. Hindus and Sikhs are cremated.

Habib Salih bin Alawi, who studied on the island and founded Riyadah Mosque-College there in 1889.

Family Celebrations

Kenyan families celebrate their own special times and are especially joyous at the birth of a baby. In traditional villages, midwives attend the expectant mother and then bury the afterbirth in a nearby field to bring good luck and fertility. After being alone with the baby, the new mother introduces her child to friends.

The celebration is often one for the whole village to enjoy, with the sacrifice of a goat for the birth feast. In cities, Kenyan women are more likely to give birth in a hospital with a doctor and nurses attending. The family may host a feast a few days after the birth of their first baby, or have a christening party.

As for birthdays, Kenyan teens and younger children are likely to get a cake, with friends invited to share it. Popular gifts include books, such as a classic novel like *The Adventures of Tom Sawyer,* or maybe new clothes made by their mother. They also might go to a hotel for a rare meal outside the home or to a movie with their parents.

Kenya exports tea to more than 40 countries, including top customers Pakistan, Egypt, and the United Kingdom.

5

From Plantations to Safaris

DURING HARVEST, TEEN WORKERS ARE UP to their waists in the green tea plants. With large woven straw baskets strapped around their foreheads and hanging down their backs, they track across the hillsides of the tea plantation, picking handfuls of slender leaves to fill their baskets.

Friends and family members work together in the temperate climate of the Kenyan highlands, where most of the export crops are grown. They pass the time by talking and joking as they work. Like three out of every four Kenyan workers, they labor on the land.

In the fertile highlands of Kenya's interior, crops grown on plantations include tea and coffee. Kenya has been one of the world's biggest exporters of both. Most of the tea and coffee is sent to European countries, including the United Kingdom and the Netherlands. In 2005, Kenya exported more than 40.23 billion shillings (U.S.$567.4 million) in tea, placing it among the biggest export crops.

In recent years, Kenya has diversified its export crops to include pineapples, bananas, passion fruit, green beans, and snow peas. Kenyan produce is found in many European supermarkets now. In addition, cut flowers, including roses, lilies, and orchids, have become important export crops.

Most Kenyan teens work on their own family's farm, growing mainly the food their family needs to survive. Maize is the most important crop in the Kenyan diet. While it is sometimes eaten roasted on the cob, more often it is ground into a flour that is cooked into ugali. Depending on the climate, family farmers also grow sweet potatoes, cassava, and coconut. Families sometimes grow a cash crop, such as coffee or sugarcane, to earn money to buy tools or clothing.

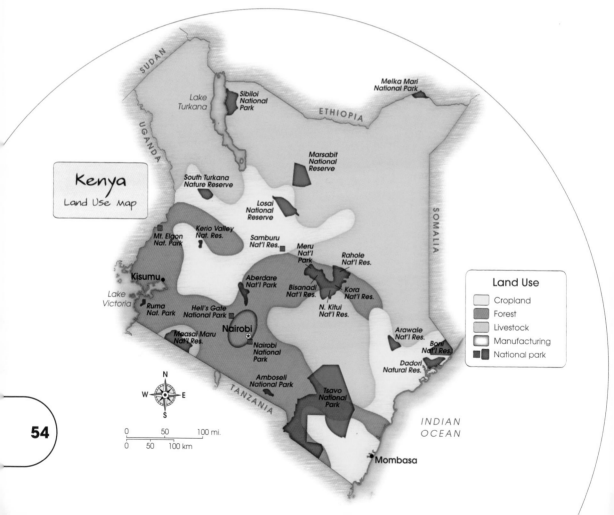

Kenya
Land Use Map

Land Use
Cropland
Forest
Livestock
Manufacturing
National park

Everything's Coming Up Roses

The flower industry in Kenya has been growing at a rapid rate—the volume and value of cut flowers exported have both increased by 35 percent annually over the past 15 years. Roses, which account for 73 percent of flower exports, are expected to see continued growth. Other exports include mixed bouquets (11 percent) and carnations (5 percent).

The Kenyan flower business accounts for 60 percent of all African flower trade and provides the countries of the European Union with 31 percent of their flower imports.

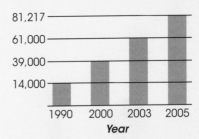

Growth of Kenya's Flower Industry

Volume exported (in tons)

81,217
61,000
39,000
14,000

1990 2000 2003 2005

Year

Source: Kenya Flower Council.

Work in the flower industry includes the processing and packaging of flowers.

55

Even though agriculture employs 75 percent of Kenyan workers, only 16.3 percent of Kenya's gross domestic product comes from agriculture. Most of the crops are grown for families to eat, not to sell.

Teens whose families are farmers often don't get to study much after school—if they attend school at all.

Instead they are likely to be picking coffee beans, milking cows, or weeding crops. Even in the cities, teens are likely to have gardening chores such as watering the family vegetable plot or hoeing to eliminate weeds. The Kenyan culture generally does not believe in paying teens an allowance for doing their chores to help the family.

A farmer and her children prepare a field to grow tomatoes as a cash crop.

Most of Kenya is too dry for commercial farming. Only about 15 percent of the country, or 21.5 million acres (8.6 million hectares), gets enough rain to grow crops. On much of the rest of the land, families may have a small plot that they water. Animals are grazed on the savannas, grasslands with scattered trees, and the scrublands, with their owners moving herds in search of water. Rarely do the pastoralists kill their goats and cattle. They keep the animals as their wealth and use the milk to make butter or

Labor Force by Occupation

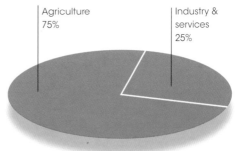

Agriculture 75%

Industry & services 25%

Source: United States Central Intelligence Agency. *The World Factbook—Kenya.*

cheese or to drink. Kenya also has a dairy industry, mostly made of small farmers who produce yogurt and cheese.

Pastoralists in northeast Kenya lost much of their herds during a devastating three-year drought starting in 2003.

Tourism Takes Off

Kenya has found that the most profitable use of much of its land is to leave it alone and preserve it for the great African animals that have lived there for thousands of years.

The nation's hottest industry is tourism. Many teens today work hard to learn about the habits of elephants, lions, cheetahs, and zebras so that they can win a job as a game tracker or a tour guide. Nairobi's Kenya Utalii College specializes in training students to work in the tourist industry.

While Europeans have been visiting Kenya for more than a century, the country's tourism industry soared after independence, when shooting animals with guns was replaced by shooting them with cameras. Today all kinds of safaris—the Kiswahili word for "journeys"—are possible, from budget camping safaris to luxury custom safaris. Many visitors hope to see the "big five" on their safari: the elephant, rhinoceros, lion, cape buffalo, and leopard.

Like other African countries blessed with abundant large mammals, Kenya has struggled with poachers, who

In 2005, 1.68 million foreign tourists visited Kenya.

kill animals for their meat, hides, or—in the case of elephants and rhinos—tusks. Antipoaching efforts have increased in recent years, as have efforts to provide alternatives in tourism-related industries to native people. For example, the Kenya Wildlife Service (KWS) encourages people living near the parks and wildlife preserves to set up lodges and shops and to offer tourists services, such as taking them on walking safaris in the bush.

Arts & Crafts

One of the ways that people living near wildlife preserves can benefit from international visitors is by selling handmade crafts. Sales of baskets woven from grasses, hand-carved wooden animals, and beaded jewelry bring villagers cash for the things they need to buy.

Kenya is famous for its soapstone carvings, and several thousand of the Kisii people, who live where the pink stone is found, earn their living carving the soft stone. Most of the sculptures are made in the shape of animals and sold to tourists. The stone is also used to make plates, boxes, and other objects.

Some artisans throughout Kenya belong to cooperatives, whose members help one another succeed. These co-ops belong to the Kenya Crafts Cooperative Union, which is endorsed by the government.

Popular Parks

Kenya's 50 national parks and reserves include:

Amboseli National Park

Famous for big game including elephants, lions, and cheetahs

Hell's Gate National Park

One of only three national parks where visitors can walk in the park, rather than ride in a vehicle

Nairobi National Park

The nation's first national park

Samburu National Reserve

Home to more than 365 species of birds

Tsavo National Park

Home to more elephants than any other place in Kenya

In 1987, tourism began bringing in more foreign money than coffee and tea, making it the number-one industry. Before the 1980s, most of the investment and profits were made by outsiders. But since then, there has been a greater effort to make sure that native people, such as the Maasai, benefit when visitors come to their traditional lands. The Maasai Mara Game Reserve is one example. The park is among the most famous places in the world for seeing the great African mammals. The dry savannas on the Serengeti plains are home to migrating animals.

To attract tourists, the government has updated facilities at Lake Nakuru National Park, home to a quarter of the world's flamingoes.

Man Versus Beast

Not all Kenyans are thrilled with the conservation of wild animals. When an elephant wrecks your garden or a lion kills your goat, it's hard to be very happy. While it is illegal to kill wildlife in Kenya, some farmers and herders feel they have no choice. In southern Kenya, the Maasai have struggled with livestock losses caused by lions. In less than two years, Partimo Ole Mereru Shoop, a 44-year-old father of 10, lost two cows and a donkey to lions, costing him more than 20,000 shillings (about U.S.$280)—an enormous amount in a country where many live on less than U.S.$1 per day.

"It made me want to poison (the lions) and get rid of them all," he said. "It's not good to kill the lions, but we never get compensation (for livestock losses), so what alternative is there?"

Though Shoop says he has not killed lions himself, others have. Since 2001, more than 100 lion killings have been recorded in his area.

A herdsman examines the carcass of a cow that was killed by a lion.

More than a million wildebeests and zebras cross the border between Tanzania and Kenya during the annual migration.

Many tourists are drawn to the park during the Kenyan winter, in July and August, to witness the annual migration of the wildebeests and zebras.

Kenya's coastal resorts have become popular with European tourists who prefer the white sand beaches and swaying palm trees to the sights of elephants and lions.

Despite the popularity of Kenya's parks and beaches, tourism suffered in the years around the millennium. In 1998, terrorists bombed the U.S. Embassy in the capital city of Nairobi, killing more than 200 people and sending visitor numbers tumbling.

More terrorist attacks occurred in 2002 in the busy seaside port of Mombasa. A tourist hotel was bombed, as was an airplane taking off from the airport. Since then, the United States has closed its embassy several times. Additionally, in the middle of the 2000s, Kenya was suffering from a severe drought, which threatened thousands of people and animals.

Though tourism is bouncing back, industry leaders face new challenges to make tourism responsible. That means returning money earned at parks and reserves to surrounding communities by investing in schools and health care facilities. And it means trying to preserve the remaining wildlife while not overrunning their homes with Land Rovers filled with tourists!

Moving to the Cities

More and more Kenyans are leaving the land for the cities, in a trend seen around the world. Part of the reason is that families traditionally divide their land among the sons—and small plots have been divided to the point where there isn't enough land left. Some teens leave for a better education in the cities, and others leave for more opportunity for different kinds of work.

Kenya has more manufacturing than many African countries, and it exports goods such as petroleum products and cement. The country also processes foods into canned goods and makes products from metals, leather, rubber, and plastic. In the cities, young people who have graduated from high school or dropped out before finishing might get a job in one of these factories or work in an office for the government or for private business.

An alarming number of people in the cities can't find jobs. The unemployment rate in 2001 was estimated at 40 percent. But this doesn't stop the enterprising Kenyans. Millions of them start their own small businesses, called *jua kali*, which means "hot sun" in Kiswahili. Most

jua kali
(JEW-ah KAH-lee)

Textile production is a common source of factory jobs.

Many Kenyans buy their clothing from private tailors or dressmakers, creating a need for the workers.

of these businesses are started outdoors by someone who has some tools and begins offering services.

For example, a young man might start a barbershop on the street by offering shaves and haircuts with clippers he bought. A woman might start a hairdressing shop with a few tools. Or a seamstress might set up shop as a tailor, repairing and even making clothes on the street. Eventually some of these businesses grow to have homes out of the hot sun.

In 2001, a survey found that the informal sector employed 4.1 million Kenyans and was responsible for more than 18 percent of the nation's gross domestic product.

Another independent means of earning money is performing on the streets. Musicians, dancers, jugglers, and mimes can all be found on the streets of cities, hoping to earn a few coins to buy dinner. Restaurants and clubs also employ some street musicians, as do major hotels.

While Kenya's economy has struggled in recent years for many reasons, there are signs that things may be improving with President Mwai Kibaki's promises to tackle corruption and improve the economic climate. In 2005, the gross domestic product grew more than 5 percent.

Struggles of a Young Government

Since independence, Kenyans have faced corruption by government leaders. Under Jomo Kenyatta, the Kikuyu people were favored, government corruption became common, and political and ethnic tensions rose. When Kenyatta died in 1978, Vice President Daniel arap Moi took over.

During the 1980s, he consolidated his power and his party. The Kenya African National Union was the only legal party for much of the decade. It became common for citizens to have to pay bribes to public officials just to get them to do their jobs. Moi had little tolerance for opposing views. Because of international pressure against his dictatorial policies, he put in place some reforms in the 1990s, but he ended up staying in power for 24 years.

In 2002, opposition candidate and former economics professor Mwai Kibaki won a landslide victory with his National Rainbow Coalition of opposition parties, and he promised reform. While there is some evidence that bribery and corruption have lessened, some estimates are that $1 billion was lost in graft between 2002 and 2005.

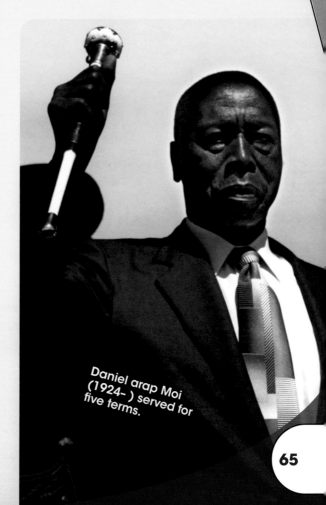

Daniel arap Moi (1924–) served for five terms.

Children of all ages enjoy playing football (soccer) together.

6

A Land of Runners & Dancers

AS SCHOOL LETS OUT in the afternoon, streams of teen boys and girls head for the fields to play the most popular sport in Kenya: football, or soccer.

The game can be played almost anywhere, and even the lack of a good ball or a real field in much of rural Kenya doesn't stop play.

A ball can be made from wound-up rags, and even a termite mound can serve as a goalpost. All over Kenya, boys and girls pursue their love of football after school.

Teens, like their elders, also like to follow professional sports and keep up with the national team, the Harambee Stars.

67

The Harambee Stars, in red, regularly compete against other African nations, such as Tunisia, in white.

Two professional football leagues play each weekend, and impressive crowds turn out to cheer their favorite teams.

Football Leads to Change

One unique story about Kenyan football comes from one of the nation's biggest slums, home to more than half a million people near Nairobi. Called Mathare, it is representative of many of the challenges facing Africa. While about three-quarters of Kenyans still live in the country, mostly in small traditional rural villages, it's increasingly difficult to earn a living or grow enough food to support families. So

Kenyans stream to big cities, especially the capital, Nairobi.

But without skills, they can't find jobs and end up in places like Mathare. There they live in ramshackle huts—made of concrete block, cardboard, or even plastic sheets—without running water, electricity, or plumbing. Young people who cannot afford to attend school are often out on the streets. Some end up begging; others end up sniffing glue and getting arrested.

In 1987, a man named Bob Munro, along with youth from the area, started the Mathare Youth Sports Association (MYSA) to provide more opportunities for the challenged youth. The founders' goals for the program were to organize sports and environmental cleanup efforts in Mathare. The first boys' league had 27 teams. Today more than 13,000 boys between 9 and 18 are playing on more than 900 teams, making it the biggest league in Africa. A girls' league started in 1992 and has grown rapidly since. The association accepts all teams wanting to play.

A Football Success Story

Fifteen-year-old Naomi Syombua faces many of the challenges of other teens in the slums. With no electricity, she is forced to do homework by candlelight, and many of her personal items have been stolen from her home. In 2006, the United Nations Children's Fund (UNICEF), featured the bright young member of MYSA on its Web site.

"They [criminals who patrol the area] have stolen my money and my clothes. When I come home, every day I find one thing missing," she said.

But Syombua's involvement with MYSA has helped her avoid much of the community's violence and drug problems.

"I have friends who have been attacked by people and been raped. Others are in bad company—they are taking drugs. But me, when I play football, I'm busy. When I play football, I feel like I can do anything."

In 2005, Cherie Blair, wife of British Prime Minister Tony Blair, visited with members of MYSA.

MYSA does more than provide an organized way to play football and sponsor environmental cleanup projects. In 1994, 25 members of the Mathare United senior football team were trained to educate other young people about AIDS. The football stars continue their outreach and education work. The organization also helps kids who have been jailed, assisting in their rehabilitation.

Kenya's Famous Runners

While football is the most popular sport for teens to play in Kenya, the country is best known internationally for another sport: distance running. Kenyan runners regularly win international marathons and other distance races.

Many of the world's greatest middle- and long-distance runners come from the highlands of Kenya near the Great Rift Valley. It is a depression formed tens of millions of years ago when part of Earth's crust sank. Its altitude is about a mile (1.6 km), which helps runners

develop strong hearts and lungs. Some of the champion runners have said that, like thousands of rural Kenyan children, they had to travel several miles each way to school every day. They grew up running.

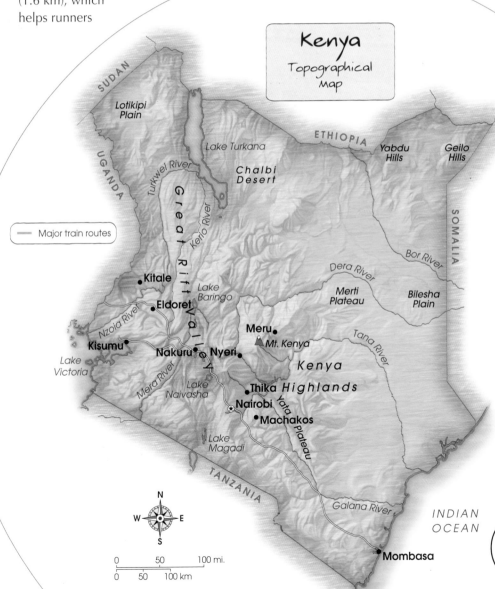

Kenya
Topographical
Map

Major train routes

Though young runners are inspired by Kip Keino's Olympic success, he considers his children's home his greatest accomplishment.

The first famous runner, and perhaps Kenya's greatest athlete of all time, is Kipchoge "Kip" Keino. He won two medals, including gold in the 1,500 meter race, at the 1968 Summer Olympics in Mexico City. In 1972, he won gold in the steeplechase, a race that involves obstacles, and set a standard of excellence in running that other Kenyans are still upholding.

A national hero, Keino, with his wife, established the Kipchoge Keino Children's Home for about 80 orphaned or abandoned children. More than 100 students have finished school there, and they all consider the Keinos their parents. The couple grows food for the home on an organic farm that also gives jobs to local people.

Kenyan women are increasingly

strong international distance runners as well. For example, Tecla Lorupe won the New York City marathon in 1994 and 1995 and placed second in the 1996 Boston marathon. Catherine Ndereba won the 2000 and 2001 Boston marathons. She is now known as "Catherine the Great."

In various parts of Kenya, teens can be seen practicing their running and other track and field events, such as hurdles and long jump, after school.

Races are commonly run across Kenyan countryside.

Neck position and movement are important features of Maasai dancing.

Song & Dance

Another form of exercise Kenyans love is dancing. Each tribe has traditional dances used to celebrate various holidays and special events. Many children learn the dances and the music that goes with them. Traditional dances often are related to ceremonies intended to bring abundant crops, good hunting, healthy families, or other goals.

Teenagers in villages still practice their traditional songs and dances, often with elaborate costumes. Dance is almost always performed to a drumbeat, which is common across the tribal groups. Another instrument—often one of several stringed instruments—plays a second beat while singers chant or sing to a third rhythm. Sometimes dancers keep the beat by wearing leg bells, as in the Boran, Embu, Kikuyu, Luo, and Maasai tribes. Dancers compete to see who can sway their hips the fastest or who can jump the highest.

In cities, teens are likely to enjoy a Kenyan form of gospel music, along with international styles, such as pop, rap, hip-hop, jazz, rhythm and blues, and rock. Kenya has developed a contemporary dance music called *benga*. Originally the rhythms were played on traditional string instruments, but now are most often played on electric guitars. Benga grew from Luo tradition and is polyrhythmic, like most African music. Most benga groups sing in Kenyan languages. Their music is most appealing to adult Kenyans.

Another form of music that came from Kenyan tradition is called *taarab*, which comes from the Kiswahili word for "enchantment." Associated with Muslims along the coastal areas, taarab music is sung by women. The songs often involve stories of romance. This musical form seems to be making a resurgence in the cities.

Teens who live in the cities are likely to go to nightclubs to hear contemporary rap or urban pop music. Singer Eric Wainaina is popular, as

benga
(ben-GUH)

taarab
(ta-AY-rab)

One of Eric Wainaina's most popular songs criticized government corruption.

are the rappers Nameless and his wife, Wahu. Many teens like to listen to the same music that's popular in Europe and the United States. Kenyan teens feel a special fondness for black American culture and music.

Reading, Watching, & Listening

When it comes to reading, Kenya has one of Africa's strongest newspaper traditions. More than 30 magazines, journals, and daily newspapers allow teens to keep up on local, national, and international news. The *Daily Nation* claims to reach three-quarters of Kenyan newspaper readers and is considered an independent voice. The same publisher, the Nation Media Group, also publishes the Kiswahili language daily *Taifa Leo*. Kenyan teens, like their elders, enjoy the crossword puzzles in newspapers as well as books of word puzzles.

Kenyan teens also enjoy movies starring American favorites such as Denzel Washington and Brad Pitt, as well as kung fu movies and Asian films that are popular with the local Indian population. Movies in the cities cost about 350 Kenyan shillings (U.S.$5)—expensive by Kenyan standards. Sometimes trucks with electric generators take movie projectors to villages so people in rural areas can enjoy movies, too.

Teens whose families have a TV might watch for an hour an evening.

Reality TV has hit Kenya with the show Project Fame, which features musicians competing for a recording deal.

Fun & Games

In addition to crossword puzzles, young Kenyans enjoy a number of other games. Girls like to play a traditional kind of jacks with stones or berries, and a form of checkers, often using homemade pieces. Modern Kenyan teens play poker and other card games. Chess is increasing in popularity as competitions increase. Board games such as Scrabble and Monopoly are played in urban areas, and teens with computers at home like to play educational computer games.

A popular traditional game is called mancala, which comes from an ancient board game. Two players face one another on either side of a board into which rows of cups are carved. Pebbles (or sometimes seeds or shells) are placed in each cup, and the players take turns moving their pebbles around, capturing their opponent's pebbles according to the rules. The loser is the first to run out of pebbles.

Younger Kenyan children make their own toys out of anything that's handy. For example, a wire clothes hanger can be used to make a toy car. In Nairobi, boys race their cars down neighborhood streets in their own "safari rally," imitating a famous car race called the Safari Rally, which brings some of the world's best road rally drivers to Kenya.

Mancala is a favorite pastime throughout Kenya.

Satellites beam in programming that includes movies, sitcoms, and dramas from Australia, Britain, the United States, and South Africa. Kenya has eight television stations, led by the state-owned Kenya Broadcasting Corporation, with programs in English and Kiswahili. Its programming largely consists of reruns of American shows and government-controlled news. In 1990, the Kenya Television Network started up in Nairobi. It brought some freedom to television news, carrying CNN news and more critical stories about the government. Nation TV, owned by the publishers of the *Daily Nation*, is based in Nairobi and carries popular shows from around the world.

Radios are the most popular way for Kenyans to enjoy music and to hear the news. Teens in Nairobi listen to Kiss FM, Capital FM, and other stations playing contemporary tunes. Radio broadcasts are reaching out to more and more of the countryside, bringing international news to rural citizens.

Not all Kenyans want to expand access to these outside cultures. Just as the nation asserted its cultural heritage in fighting for independence from the British, many Kenyans today are trying to focus on their native culture. For example, radio stations are giving more airtime to local bands. And in Nairobi, more people are mainstreaming the wearing of traditional clothing such as the kangas, the colorful rectangular

A young Kenyan woman wears a kanga as a shawl over her modern clothing.

cotton cloths that women tie around their waists like a skirt and sometimes around their head and shoulders as well.

A Nation of Storytellers

Many Kenyan teens who live in the countryside have never heard of any of the American movie stars or hip-hop bands. They have no electricity, much less a television in their home. Girls walk miles every day to fetch water and wood for the fire so the family can eat dinner. They are usually looking after little brothers and sisters, too. Boys, meanwhile, are likely to be working in the fields with their fathers to grow the grain they grind for their porridge, or they are keeping track of the cattle herds.

But that doesn't mean they don't enjoy leisure time and culture. Kenyans are great storytellers, and it is only in about the last 40 years that Kenyans have written down many of their stories or started writing books as we know them.

In the countryside, young people learn about the traditions of their culture by listening to stories. Many of them are fables that teach a moral lesson, often through the stories of one animal that outsmarts another one. In some villages, families gather after dinner at the home of the best storyteller, often a grandmother. She mimics the various animals and sometimes asks the young people to play characters, so the storytelling is almost like a play. Many Kenyans believe that the spirits of their ancestors can still be contacted, so some of the stories are about ways that the dead family members can come and help the living.

Kenyan parents also tell their children proverbs that have been passed down through the generations. For example: "He who is unable to dance says that the yard is stony." The lesson is: Don't make excuses for things you can't do. Another is "Hurrying has no blessing."

An important time for young people to learn the stories of their history is during initiation into adulthood.

A National Hero

Traditional storytellers inspired Kenya's best-known writer and first novelist, Ngugi wa Thiong'o. His first book, *Weep Not, Child,* was a novel in English about a Kikuyu family during Kenya's struggle for independence. Since it was published, in 1966, he has used Kenya's political struggles as inspiration.

His most famous book, *Petals of Blood,* also in English, was written in 1977. The book was a criticism of the society. It contrasted the struggles of poor Kenyans in rural areas with corrupt government officials who are wealthy.

That same year, Ngugi decided to stop writing in English and write only in Gikuyu (the native language of the Kikuyu) or Kiswahili to reach more Kenyans. His play *I Will Marry When I Want* was produced at a Kikuyu community center with people talking in their own language. The result? The play angered government officials, and Ngugi was put in jail for a year. When he got out, he wrote *Mother Sing to Me,* a Kikuyu play that shed light on government corruption and injustice. His work in Kikuyu was banned in Kenya, and Ngugi had to move to England in 1982 to avoid being jailed again.

The government interference with writers put a damper on Kenyan literature in the 1980s and 1990s. But a new generation of writers emerged in the 2000s. In 2002, one of the best-known Kenyan writers, Binyavanga Wainaina, received the prestigious Caine Prize for African Writing. His short story "Discovering Home" explores his feelings about returning to Kenya after living in South Africa for 10 years.

Author Ngugi wa Thiong'o is internationally acclaimed.

FREEDOM OF EXPRESSION FOR EVERYONE

Amnesty International
PROTECT THE HUMAN

Schoolchildren enjoy visiting Nairobi Park's animal orphanage, where sick, injured, or abandoned animals are rehabilitated for release into the park.

Giving Back

Many Kenyan teens dedicate some of their leisure time to their country's most famous asset—its wildlife. More than 50,000 Kenyans, most of them school-children, belong to the Wildlife Clubs of Kenya (WCK), an organization started in 1968 by Richard Leakey, a famous paleontologist whose family discovered some of the earliest human remains in Kenya.

The clubs, usually based in schools, are registered with the Kenya Wildlife Service. Members pay a fee to gain free entrance to all the KWS areas and parks and go on organized trips to see wildlife. They also help take care of animals, learn at study centers in parks, and make bird feeders.

Even those who do not belong to the WCK are likely to spend some time in nature. Schools generally try to intro-duce their students to wildlife parks.

Sometimes a visit to a famous park, such as Maasai Mara, is the reward for a team of students who win a provincial contest in an academic topic. Other times, schools take field trips to parks or wildlife centers nearby. A favorite of many students is the snake park in the national museum in Nairobi. Today's Kenyan teens are growing up aware that the future of their country's precious wildlife will soon be in their hands.

81

Looking Ahead

KENYA IS THE CENTER OF FINANCE AND TRADE FOR EAST AFRICA, WITH MORE MANUFACTURING AND BETTER TRANSPORTATION AND COMMUNICATION FACILITIES THAN MANY OF ITS NEIGHBORS. But in recent years, the nation has faced huge challenges. The 24-year reign of President Moi was marred by corruption that put a damper on the whole economy. Severe droughts have hurt agriculture and threatened people with starvation. And AIDS has cut the average lifespan by nearly a decade.

Kenyan teens face significant challenges. How do they accept modern ideas without losing the values of their traditional cultures? How will they feed a growing population in a country where most of the land is not arable and rains are not reliable? Can they create enough jobs for the growing population?

Their challenges will play out in an increasingly international arena, a world in which young people from all over will be sharing information via the Internet in ways their elders could not imagine. The future of Kenyan teens will be closely linked to that of teenagers around the world.

At a Glance

Official name: Republic of Kenya

Capital: Nairobi

People

Population: 34,707,817

Population by age group:
0–14 years: 42.6%
15–64 years: 55.1%
65 years and over: 2.3%

Life expectancy at birth: 48.9 years

Official languages: Kiswahili and English

Religions:
Protestant: 45%
Roman Catholic: 33%
Indigenous beliefs: 10%
Muslim: 10%
Other: 2%

Legal ages:
Alcohol consumption: 18
Driver's license: 18
Employment in agriculture or service:
no minimum
Employment in industry: 16
Marriage: Following puberty or initiation
Military service: 18
Voting: 18

Government

Type of government: Republic

Chief of state: President, elected by popular vote

Head of government: President, elected by popular vote

Lawmaking body: Mbunge (National Assembly), elected by popular vote

Administrative divisions: Seven provinces and one area

Independence: December 12, 1963 (from United Kingdom)

National symbols: The colors of the Kenyan flag are each symbolic. Black represents the people of Kenya, red represents the struggle for freedom, green represents agriculture and natural resources, and white represents unity and peace. The flag's shield symbolizes the defense of freedom.

Geography

Total Area: 233,060 square miles (582,650 square kilometers)

Climate: Straddles equator; varies from tropical along coast to arid in interior

Highest point: Mount Kenya, 17,157 feet (5,199 meters)

Lowest point: Indian Ocean, sea level

Major rivers & lakes: Tana, Galana rivers; Lake Turkana, Lake Victoria

Major landforms: Bilesha Plain, Chalbi Desert, Gello Hills, Great Rift Valley, Kenya Highlands, Lotikipi Plain, Merti Plateau, Mount Kenya, Yata Plateau

Economy

Currency: Kenyan shilling

Population below poverty line: 50%

Major natural resources: Limestone, soda ash, salt, gemstones, fluorite, zinc, diatomite, gypsum, wildlife

Major agricultural products: Flowers, tea, coffee, corn, wheat, sugarcane, fruit, vegetables, dairy products, beef, pork, poultry, eggs

Major exports: Tea, horticultural products, coffee, petroleum products, fish, cement

Major imports: Machinery and transportation equipment, petroleum products, motor vehicles, iron and steel, resins, plastics

Historical Timeline

Portugal, then a major colonial power, claims the coastal areas of east Africa, including Kenya

Native Kenyans create the Kenyan African National Union to work toward independence, whil[e] much of the world is embroiled in World War II (1939–1945)

Arabs begin settling coastal areas

 British colonies are established in North America

East African Protectorat[e] which is run by a Britis[h] governor, becomes crown colony of Kenya

| 2000 B.C. | 600 A.D. | 1489 | 1500–1600 | 1600s | 1888 | 1914–1918 | 1920 | 1944 |

Cushite settlers move from the north to what is now Kenya

 World War I

First European exploration begins when Portuguese Vasco de Gama visits what is now the Kenyan port of Mombasa

Imperial British East Africa Co. founded, signaling the beginning of British claim to Kenya

86  Historical World Event

British declare a state of emergency because of the Mau Mau rebellion against British rule; leaders, including Jomo Kenyatta, are jailed

Kenya gains its independence; Kenyatta elected president the following year

The government suppresses opposition groups; political arrests and human-rights abuses fire international criticism

 The first personal computer in the world is introduced

1950–1953   1952   1956   1961   1963   1978   1981   1987

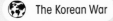 The Korean War

 Soviet cosmonaut is the first human to enter space

Mau Mau rebellion is put down after thousands, mostly Africans, are killed

Kenyatta dies and is recognized as Mzee—"the wise old one"—by his people and many world leaders; he is succeeded by Daniel arap Moi

Historical Timeline

A continuing severe drought in the Horn of Africa is leading to the threat of thousands of people starving as famine spreads across parts of Kenya

The HIV/AIDS epidemic is declared a national disaster

2,000 people are killed in a tribal conflict in the western part of the country

The economy grows more than 5 percent, in a year, showing that efforts to take on the problems of corruption seem to be working

Soviet Union collapses

1989   1991   1992   1998   1999   2002   2005   2006

Famed paleontologist Richard Leakey is named the head of the Kenya Wildlife Service, and a major crackdown on the poaching that is decimating the nation's prized animals begins

After 24 years in power, during which he won elections marred by fraud and violence, Moi is succeeded by Mwai Kibaki, a candidate of the National Rainbow Coalition who promises to crack down on corruption

A truck bomb explodes near the U.S. Embassy in downtown Nairobi, killing 213 people; the United States blames it on al Qaeda, the same terrorist group that will be blamed for the September 11, 2001, attacks in the United States

Glossary

AIDS | abbreviation for Acquired Immune Deficiency Syndrome, a disease of the immune system that makes people more likely to catch infections and some rare cancers that are often fatal; usually transmitted by sexual activity or contaminated blood

arable | fit for or used for the growing of crops

circumcision | surgical removal of part of the reproductive organs; in males, the foreskin of the penis is removed, and in females, part or all of the clitoris is removed

graft | unethical practices, such as bribery, used to make gains in politics or business

gross domestic product | the total value of all goods and services produced in a country

impoverished | living in a state of poverty

indigenous | native to a place

informal sector | work or businesses that are not regulated by a government; information about income and employment in the informal sector are usually not gathered

kangas | colorful cotton cloths that Kenyan women traditionally wrap around their waists like a skirt

pastoralists | people who raise herds of animals

polyrhythmic | music that features combinations of contrasting rhythms

provincial | related to the provinces, Kenya's administrative divisions

vocational | referring to a particular field of employment, usually a field that requires skilled workers such as mechanics, plumbers, or carpenters

Additional Resources

IN THE LIBRARY

Bowden, Rob. *The Changing Face of Kenya*. Chicago: Raintree Steck-Vaughn, 2003.

Broberg, Catherine. *Kenya in Pictures*. Minneapolis: Lerner Publications Co., 2003.

Corrigan, Jim. *Kenya*. Philadelphia: Mason Crest Publishers, 2005.

Falola, Toyin, ed. *Teen Life in Africa*. Westport, Conn.: Greenwood Press, 2004.

Giles, Bridget. *Kenya*. Austin: Raintree Steck-Vaughn, 2002.

Lemasolai-Lekuton, Joseph. *Facing the Lion: Growing Up Maasai on the African Savanna*. Washington, D.C.: National Geographic, 2003.

Pateman, Robert. *Kenya*. New York: Benchmark Books, 2004.

ON THE WEB

For more information on this topic, use FactHound.

1. Go to *www.facthound.com*
2. Type in this book ID: 0756524458
3. Click on the *Fetch It* button.

Look for more Global Connections books.

Teens in Australia

Teens in Brazil

Teens in China

Teens in France

Teens in India

Teens in Israel

Teens in Japan

Teens in Mexico

Teens in Russia

Teens in Saudi Arabia

Teens in Spain

Teens in Venezuela

Teens in Vietnam

Source Notes

Page 15, column 1, line 4: Victor Chinyama. "Kenya's Abolition of School Fees Offers Lessons for Rest of Africa." UNICEF. 17 April 2006. 8 Aug. 2006. www.unicef.org/infobycountry/kenya_33391.html

Page 18, column 1, line 14: Nicole Leistikow. "Teen Girls Flooding Kenya's New No-Cost Schools." *Women's eNews*. 7 Sept. 2003. 8 Aug. 2006. http://womensenews.org/article.cfm/dyn/aid/1516/

Page 36, column 1, line 10: "Caroline's Story." Teenage Mothers & Girls Association of Kenya. January 2006. 21 Sept. 2006. www.afrikapamoja.org/temak/caroline_story.htm

Page 41, column 1, line 27: Malini Morzaria and Zeinab Ahmed. "Education and Awareness Make Progress Against Female Genital Cutting in Kenya." UNICEF. 24 Aug. 2006. 17 Nov. 2006. www.unicef.org/infobycountry/kenya_35433.html

Page 61, line 16: Rob Crilly. "Southern Kenya's Masai Tribe, Lions Locked in Battle." *USA Today*. 30 Aug. 2006. 19 Sept. 2006. www.usatoday.com/news/world/2006-08-30-lions_x.htm

Page 69, column 1, line 10: Thomas Nybo. "Naomi Siombua, 15, Builds Confidence Playing Football in a Kenyan Slum." UNICEF. 2006. 19 Sept. 2006. www.unicef.org/football/index_intro_33941.html

Page 79, column 2, line 12: "Kenyan Proverbs." World of Quotes. 2003–2006. 20 Sept. 2006. www.worldofquotes.com/proverb/Kenyan/1/index.html

Pages 84–85, At a Glance: United States. Central Intelligence Agency. *The World Factbook—Kenya*. 17 Oct. 2006. 31 Oct. 2006. www.cia.gov/cia/publications/factbook/geos/ke.html

Select Bibliography

Atwood, Melinda. *Jambo, Mama.* Fort Bragg, Calif.: Cypress House, 2001.

"Caroline's Story." Teenage Mothers & Girls Association of Kenya. January 2006. 21 Sept. 2006. www.afrikapamoja.org/temak/caroline_story.htm

Chinyama, Victor. "Kenya's Abolition of School Fees Offers Lessons for Rest of Africa." UNICEF. 17 April 2006. 8 Aug. 2006. www.unicef.org/infobycountry/kenya_33391.html

"Country Profile: Kenya." *BBC News.* 19 July 2006. 8 Sept. 2006. http://news.bbc.co.uk/2/hi/africa/country_profiles/1024563.stm

Crilly, Rob. "Southern Kenya's Masai Tribe, Lions Locked in Battle." *USA Today.* 30 Aug. 2006. 19 Sept. 2006. www.usatoday.com/news/world/2006-08-30-lions_x.htm

Daily Nation Online. 8 Sept. 2006. www.nationaudio.com

Finke, Jens. "The Traditional Music and Cultures of Kenya." *BlueGecko.org.* 2000–2003. 8 Sept. 2006. www.bluegecko.org/kenya

"Floriculture in Kenya." Kenya Flower Council. 9 Nov. 2006. www.kenyaflowers.co.ke/industryinfo/flori.php

The Green Belt Movement. 8 Sept. 2006. www.greenbeltmovement.org/

Harman, Danna. "No-Fee Plan Floods Kenya Schools." *The Christian Science Monitor.* 21 Jan. 2003. 8 Sept. 2006. www.csmonitor.com/2003/0121/p06s01-woaf.html

"Kenya." *Africa Online*. 8 Sept. 2006. www.Africaonline.co.ke

Kenya Association of Tour Operators. 8 Sept. 2006. www.katokenya.org/

"Kenya: Life Expectancy at Birth." UN Common Database. Globalis–Kenya. 9 Nov. 2006. http://globalis.gvu.unu.edu/ indicator_detail.cfm?Country=KE&Indic atorID=18#row

The Kenya Tourist Board. 7 Sept. 2006. http://magicalkenya.com

Kenya Wildlife Service. 8 Sept. 2006. www.kws.org

"Kenyan Proverbs." World of Quotes. 2003–2006. 20 Sept. 2006. www. worldofquotes.com/proverb/Kenyan/1/ index.html

Kenyan Society UK. 8 Sept. 2006. www.kenyansociety.co.uk/index.htm

Kenyaweb: Kenya's Internet Resource. 7 Sept. 2006. http://www.kenyaweb.com/

Leistikow, Nicole. "Teen Girls Flooding Kenya's New No-Cost Schools." *Women's eNews* 7 Sept. 2003. 8 Aug. 2006. http://womensenews.org/article. cfm/dyn/aid/1516/

Mathare Youth Sports Association. 9 Sept. 2006. http://mysakenya.org/

Morzaria, Malini, and Zeinab Ahmed. "Education and Awareness Make Progress Against Female Genital Cutting in Kenya." UNICEF. 24 Aug. 2006. 17 Nov. 2006. www.unicef.org/ infobycountry/kenya_35433.html

National Geographic. *Africa: Whatever You Thought, Think Again. Special Issue*. September 2005. 25 Sept. 2006. http://www7.nationalgeographic.com/ ngm/0509/

Nybo, Thomas. "Naomi Siombua, 15, Builds Confidence Playing Football in a Kenyan Slum." UNICEF. 2006. 19 Sept. 2006. www.unicef.org/football/index_ intro_33941.html

Press, Robert M. *The New Africa: Dispatches from a Changing Continent*. Gainesville, Fla.: University Press of Florida, 1999.

United States. Central Intelligence Agency. *The World Factbook—Kenya*. 17 Oct. 2006. 31 Oct. 2006. www. cia.gov/cia/publications/factbook/geos/ ke.html

Index

About the Author
Rebecca Cantwell

Rebecca Cantwell is a freelance writer and editor in Denver, Colorado. She worked for many years as a reporter and editor for major newspapers and magazines. She has traveled extensively and journeyed to southern Africa in 2006 on safari. She found the people, the animals, and the land of Africa as magical as she had imagined.

About the Content Adviser
Angela N. Mwenda, M.Env.Sc.

Angela N. Mwenda lectures on geography and environmental sciences at Christ the Teacher Institute for Education at Tangaza College, which is the Nairobi campus of St. Mary's University of Minnesota. In reviewing the book for the second time, she commented, "[The changes] give a fuller picture and the book is now very catchy! Many of the photographs make me smile, as they show aspects of Kenya that very few people know about!"